Long Time No See

MIKE WILSON

The
Basic Skills

I don't go out on a Thursday night.
Normally.
But that Thursday night, I did.

Normally, I get home,
and I'm too tired.

I can't be bothered.

But then – from time to time,
you feel like a bit of company,
don't you?

I stopped seeing Sharon,
my ex,
about ten months ago.

Or rather,
she stopped seeing me.

Sometimes it gets me down.
I get fed up.
Lonely.

But then I think to myself:
come on Dennis,
pull yourself together!

If you stop in all the time,
on your own,
what will happen?

Nothing, that's what!

So, this Thursday night,
I go down the pub.

I'm looking for adventure!

There's music on.
The place is full of people.

People talking.
People singing.
People drinking
and having a good time.

As soon as I go in,
I begin to feel better.

I get myself a pint,
and have a good look round.

There's a big gang of women
over in the corner.

Some of them turn and look at me.

Then I hear a scream,
and one of the women comes running over,
and she's shouting "Dennis! Dennis!"

and she puts her arms round me
and gives me a big wet kiss!

"Dennis!" she says,
"Don't you remember me?
It's Lesley, remember?"

She's holding on to me for dear life.

"Oh, yes!" I say, "Lesley!
Long time no see!
When was it? Two years ago?"

"More like three," she says.

She sips her sweet Martini.
Her eyes are shining.

She says:
"God, it's so good to see you!"
and she hugs me and kisses me again.

I can't tell:
is she just very drunk?

Or is she really this pleased to see me?

A woman comes over and says:
"Lesley, are you all right?"

"Oh Mary! Mary!" says Lesley,
"Come and meet Dennis!
He's a builder.

"He did some work
on a house I lived in
a few years ago.

"I really fancied him, Mary,
but I never told him!

"It's ages since I saw him!

"And now, tonight,
we bump into each other!
Tonight of all nights!"

Did I really hear that right?
Did Lesley say she fancied me,
all those years ago?

Fancied me?

Lesley leans close to me.

She says:
"All my friends say
I must try and get off with a man tonight!"

Then she giggles,
and takes a swig of sweet Martini.

I hear the glass hit her teeth.

But then her friend Mary puts her arm
between us
and leads Lesley away.

"Sorry to bother you," Mary says,
over her shoulder to me,
"Lesley's had a few...you know!"

"Oh it's no bother," I say,
"No bother at all!"

I'm thinking:
I like being bothered like this,
even by a woman I hardly know!

They go and sit in the corner.

Two seconds later, Lesley's back.

"I'm so sorry!" she says.

She holds on to my arm.
I can feel her sway into me.
So close.

"Sorry, sorry, sorry!" she says again.
She looks up at me.
"I shouldn't have done all that, Dennis.
I'm just drunk, so just ignore me!

"And anyway," she goes on,
"you had a girlfriend, didn't you?
What was her name again?
I bet you're still seeing her, aren't you?"

"Oh no! No no no no," I say.
"No, that's all over.
Ages ago. Months.
Don't you worry about that!"

I look down.
Then, quietly, I say:
"Sharon. Her name was Sharon."

When I go red,
it's always my ears.

They go all hot and bright red.
They look like two poppies,
sticking out of the side of my head.

And I'm just standing there,
looking at my shoes,
hoping Lesley will still fancy me
with ears sticking out like two poppies.

But Lesley has gone.
Again.

Mary is leading her away again,
back to the other women in the corner.

Mary is saying:
"Come on, Lesley! Come away!
Leave the lad alone!
He doesn't want you all over him!"

Oh, but I do.
I do.

They go and sit down again,
and talk for a bit.

One or two of the other women
look over at me.
Once, Lesley smiles and waves.

And then, nothing much happens
for another ten minutes.

I don't know what else to do,
so I just go and get myself another pint.

I'm at the bar,
when I feel a tap on my arm.

She's back.

I smile and turn round.

But it's only Mary.

Mary says:
"I just wanted to say sorry again.
For Lesley, you know,
being a bother."

"Oh, it's no bother," I say again,
"I feel like a bit of company.
We're old friends, me and Lesley.
We fancied one another for ages!"

"But I must explain,"
Mary goes on.
"I don't want Lesley to do anything...
you know...stupid. Tonight.

"She's very very drunk,
and she's a bit...reckless.
I didn't want you to get the wrong idea...

"You see, Dennis,
this is Lesley's Hen Party tonight.
She gets married on Saturday.

"And we don't want anything
to spoil the best day of her life,
do we?"